CUENTO
DE LUZ

Adriel, Marc and Yuna, don't be afraid. I love you

- Susanna Isern -

What Are You Scared of, Little Mouse?

Text © Susanna Isern
Illustrations © Nora Hilb
This edition © 2015 Cuento de Luz SL
Calle Claveles 10 | Urb. Monteclaro | Pozuelo de Alarcón | 28223 | Madrid | Spain
www.cuentodeluz.com
Title in Spanish: *¿De qué tienes miedo, Ratoncito?*
English translation by Jon Brokenbrow

ISBN: 978-84-15784-68-5

Printed by Shanghai Chenxi Printing Co., Ltd. January 2015, print number 1477-2

FSC
www.fsc.org
MIX
Paper from
responsible sources
FSC® C007923

What Are You Scared of, Little Mouse?

Susanna Isern & Nora Hilb

Lately, Little Mouse is very **scared**.
He feels frightened all the time,
and is afraid of everything.
Mommy Mouse is very worried.

Very early in the morning, he wakes up with a start.

"What are you scared of, Little Mouse?"

"I'm afraid of the **dark**, in case a monster comes and gets me."

"Look around you, Little Mouse. There aren't any monsters in your room. You're just imagining things."

In the summer, he doesn't swim in the lake.

"What are you scared of, Little Mouse?"

"I'm afraid of the **water** and the **bugs** swimming around in it."

"Look at the frogs, Little Mouse. They're happy and their tummies are full. If there were any bugs, they've already eaten them."

When they're in the forest, he hides in a hollow tree trunk.

"What are you scared of, Little Mouse?"

"I'm afraid the **owl** might come along and snatch me up in his claws."

"Look at the sun shining, Little Mouse. The owl is asleep in his nest. Listen carefully and you can hear him snoring."

If he gets a sniffle, he worries too much.

"What are you scared of, Little Mouse?"

"I'm afraid of **being sick**, and not being able to play with my friends."

"Just look at yourself, Little Mouse. You're strong and healthy. Tomorrow you'll be all better."

When they go out for a walk, he doesn't run off and play.
"What are you scared of, Little Mouse?"
"I'm afraid I might **get lost**, and never see you again."
"Look at my eyes, Little Mouse. Even though they're tiny, they're always watching you. You're never out of sight."

When they go to pick hazelnuts, he doesn't climb the trees.

"What are you scared of, Little Mouse?"

"I'm afraid of **falling out** of the tree and bumping my head."

"Look at all the leaves on the ground, Little Mouse. If you did fall down, it would be like landing on a feather bed."

Some days, he goes to school with his tail between his legs.

"What are you scared of, Little Mouse?"

"I'm afraid **no one will talk to me** because I'm scared of everything."

"Look at your classmates, Little Mouse. They're just having fun. If you ask them to play, you'll have a wonderful time."

At home he's frightened,
and doesn't want to be left alone.
    "What are you scared of,
Little Mouse?"
    "I'm afraid the cat
might come along and stick
his whiskers through the window."
    "Look at our nest, Little Mouse.
We're hidden away in the ground,
amongst the roots and under the stones."

When there's a storm, he hides
under his bed and covers his ears.
"What are you scared of, Little Mouse?"
"I'm afraid of the **thunder** and lightning."
"Look at the water falling from the sky,
Little Mouse. The flowers are all dancing
in the rain, and the thunder is their music."

"You see? There's nothing to be scared of."
"You're right, Mommy. You know, there's really only one thing I'm afraid of."

"What are you scared of, Little Mouse?"
"I'm afraid of you not being by my side,
to give me a great big hug."
"Don't be afraid, Little Mouse. I'm here.
I love you."